ROLLO and TWEEDY and the GHOST at DOUGAL CASTLE

STORY AND PICTURES BY
Laura Jean Allen

HarperCollins*Publishers*

This book is a presentation of Newfield Publications, Inc.
Newfield Publications offers book clubs for children
from preschool through high school. For further
information write to: **Newfield Publications, Inc.**
4343 Equity Drive, Columbus, Ohio 43228.

Published by arrangement with HarperCollins Publishers.
Newfield Publications is a federally registered trademark of
Newfield Publications, Inc. I Can Read Book is a
registered trademark of HarperCollins Publishers.

Library of Congress Cataloging-in-Publication Data
Allen, Laura Jean.
    Rollo and Tweedy and the ghost at Dougal Castle: story and
pictures by Laura Jean Allen.
        p.   cm.-—(An I can read book)
    Summary: Lord Dougal asks the detective Tweedy and his
assistant Rollo to solve the mystery of the ghost haunting Dougal Castle.
    ISBN 0-06-020106-1. — ISBN 0-06-020107-X. (lib. bdg.)
    [1. Castles—Fiction. 2. Ghosts — Fiction. 3. Mystery and dectective
stories.] I. Title. II. Series.
PZ7.A4274Rog 1992   89-26921
[E]—dc20   CIP
                                                                AC

The illustrations in this book are rendered in watercolor and pen and ink.

To Nina,
with many fond bouquets

"Tweedy, I need your help,"

said Lord Dougal.

"Please come at once."

Tweedy was a famous detective.

Rollo was his assistant

and best friend.

"Welcome to Scotland,"

said Lord Dougal.

"I am counting on you American lads

to solve our mystery."

"Tell us about it," said Tweedy.

"We have a castle ghost,"

said Lord Dougal.

"My granddaughter Bonnie saw it."

"The ghost walked

right past my window,"

said Bonnie.

"Who else has seen this ghost?"

asked Tweedy.

"The cook," said Bonnie,

"and the gardener."

"The chimney sweep saw it too,"

said Lord Dougal.

"It scared the shepherd,"

said Bonnie.

"All the sheep ran away."

9

"The ghost is scaring

all my servants,"

said Lord Dougal.

"Who else lives here?"

asked Rollo.

Bonnie said,

"The maid lives here, and

our housekeeper, Mrs. MacRobb,

and her husband."

"Hmmm," said Tweedy.

"Please find the ghost

before they leave!"

cried Bonnie.

"We will catch your ghost,"

said Tweedy.

"I promise you."

That night Rollo and Tweedy
hid and watched for the ghost.
"There it goes!" cried Rollo.
"Let's follow it," said Tweedy.

Rollo and Tweedy ran after the ghost.

"The ghost is gone!" cried Rollo.

"Hmmm," said Tweedy.

"This *is* a mystery."

13

The next morning Tweedy said,

"Lord Dougal, please tell us

something about the castle."

"Well," said Lord Dougal,

"the castle is very old.

There are many stories about it."

"Does the castle have secrets?"

asked Tweedy.

"There is a hidden treasure,"

said Lord Dougal,

"but it is no secret.

Everyone knows about it."

"Does everyone know

where the treasure is hidden?"

asked Tweedy.

"Oh, no!" said Lord Dougal.

"Only I know

where the treasure is."

"Hmmm," said Tweedy.

"Would you show us

around the castle?

Maybe Rollo and I

will find some clues

about your ghost."

"Of course," said Lord Dougal.

"Here is the shepherd's house,"
said Lord Dougal.

"Look!" said Rollo. "A sheet."

"It looks just like the ghost,"
said Bonnie.

"Hmmm," said Tweedy.

"What is this strange ditch?"

asked Tweedy.

"The gardener said

he is planting trees here,"

said Lord Dougal.

"Maybe it could lead

to the treasure!" said Rollo.

"Hmmm," said Tweedy.

"Let's see the kitchen."

"This way,"

said Lord Dougal.

"Look!" said Rollo. "A map!"

"Hmmm," said Tweedy.

"It is drawn

on the back of a recipe."

20

"Wow!" said Rollo.

"Maybe it is a map to the treasure!"

"Hmmm," said Tweedy.

21

"What about the chimney sweep?"

asked Tweedy.

"He is strange,"

said Lord Dougal.

"Once we found him in the library.

He said he had fallen

down the library chimney.

Oh, there he is again."

"Hmmm," said Tweedy.

That night

Rollo and Tweedy hid again.

Hours passed.

KER-CHOO!

"Shhh!" said Tweedy.

"Try not to sneeze again."

"I did not sneeze," said Rollo.

"If you did not sneeze, who did?"
asked Tweedy.

"It must have been the ghost!"
said Rollo.

"Ghosts do not sneeze," said Tweedy.

"They have no noses."

"Do ghosts have feet?"

asked Rollo.

"No," said Tweedy.

"Well, that ghost

wore big black shoes!" said Rollo.

"Hmmm," said Tweedy.

"We saw the ghost last night,"
said Rollo at breakfast.

"Or maybe we saw

someone dressed up as a ghost,"

said Tweedy.

"Why would someone do that?"
asked Lord Dougal.

"Why would someone
want to scare us?"
asked Bonnie.

"Hmmm," said Tweedy.
"Maybe the ghost
wants to scare everyone away!"

"But why?" asked Lord Dougal.
"Maybe the ghost
wants to search for the treasure
when the castle is empty,"
said Tweedy.

"What are you going to do?"

asked Lord Dougal.

"Rollo and I will trick the ghost,"

said Tweedy.

"How?" asked Bonnie.

"We will make the ghost *think*

the castle is empty,"

said Tweedy.

"Good idea," said Lord Dougal.

The next morning

everyone but Mr. and Mrs. MacRobb

left the castle

right after breakfast.

Mr. and Mrs. MacRobb stayed behind

to guard the castle.

Rollo and Tweedy

were the last to leave.

Rollo and Tweedy went to a nearby inn

and ate sandwiches for lunch.

"Poor Mrs. MacRobb," said Rollo.

"What do you mean?" asked Tweedy.

"She was so sad

when she waved good-bye,"

said Rollo.

"You mean she sniffled

and blew her nose," said Tweedy.

Tweedy jumped from his chair.

"That's it!" he cried.

"Back to the castle, Rollo!

It is time to catch our ghost!"

"We must be as quiet as a ghost,"
said Tweedy.

"Right," said Rollo. "Then what?"

"We look for the ghost,"
said Tweedy.

"Rollo, you look upstairs.

I will look downstairs."

Rollo climbed up

to the highest tower.

He looked over the edge.

"This is very high,"

said Rollo.

He got a rope

and tied the end to a pillar.

He tied the other end

around his waist.

He leaned far over the edge.

SNAP! went the rope.

Down went Rollo—

right into the moat!

Mr. MacRobb fished poor Rollo

out of the moat.

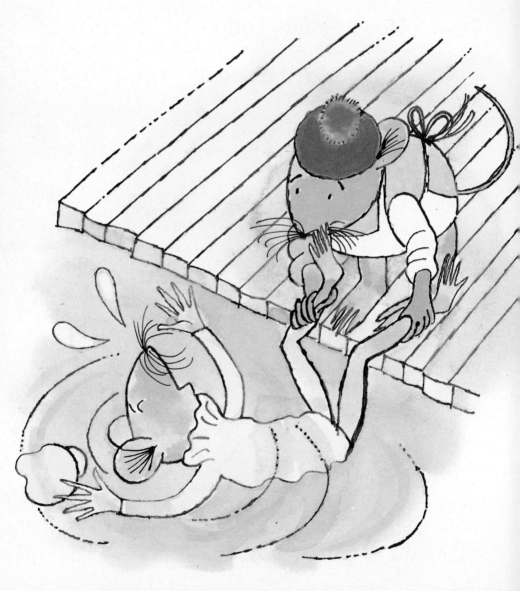

"What are you doing here?"

asked Mr. MacRobb.

"Please do not tell anyone

you saw me," said Rollo.

"Mum's the word,"

said Mr. MacRobb.

Tweedy was in the great hall.

Suddenly he heard

Ker-choo!

Tweedy turned around.

It was Rollo.

"What happened to you?"

asked Tweedy.

"I fell into the moat,"

said Rollo.

Just then they heard a loud

KER-CHOO!

It came from the library.

Tweedy opened the door slowly.

The library was empty.

"I will smoke my pipe and think,"

said Tweedy.

"The secret of a great detective

is thinking."

KER-CHOO!

"There it is again!" said Rollo.

"Hmmm—it came from the bookcase,"
said Tweedy.

"There must be

a secret door in here.

I will tap on the walls.

You listen for a hollow sound."

Tweedy began to tap

with his pipe.

He tapped each wall.

He tapped each bookcase.

Suddenly a bookcase moved.

"Look, a tunnel!" cried Rollo.

"Just as I thought," said Tweedy.

"Let's follow it."

"I see a light ahead," said Rollo.
Tweedy and Rollo moved slowly
toward the light.

51

"Aha! Our castle ghost!"

cried Tweedy.

"Drat!" said Mrs. MacRobb.

"I found the treasure.

It is mine!"

"Wrong!" said Tweedy.

"The treasure

belongs to Lord Dougal.

You are just a thief.

Your ghosting days are over."

That evening Rollo and Tweedy

had tea with Bonnie and Lord Dougal.

"Why was the ghosty sheet

in the shepherd's cottage?"

asked Bonnie.

"It *seemed* like a good clue, Bonnie,"

said Tweedy.

"But now we know

the shepherd shakes it

to frighten the wolves."

"How about the cook's map?"

asked Lord Dougal.

"Poor cook," said Tweedy.

"She often gets lost

in this big castle.

She made her own map,

so she would not get lost."

"And the ditch?" asked Lord Dougal.

"Just what the gardener said it was,"

said Tweedy.

"What about the chimney sweep?"

asked Bonnie.

"A fine lad," said Tweedy.

"He just lost his footing.

He also loves to read."

"Well, well," said Lord Dougal.

"You are a great detective,

and we thank you."

The castle was happy again.

The cook baked tarts.

The gardener planted trees.

The chimney sweep swept the chimneys.

The shepherd watched the sheep.

Lord Dougal gave a party

for Rollo and Tweedy.

"Back to America and our next case!"

said Tweedy.

"But we will never forget

you and Bonnie and your castle."

"Or the ghost who was not a ghost,"

said Rollo.